ODDISCY'S EXPRESSIONS OF SENSUAL TRUTHS

Oddiscy Quest Carter

DEDICATION

To you. This book is dedicated to you.

Oh

Yeah

I dedicate this book to every living character I see and interact with during the course of any given day. While any one individual did not inspire this book and all stories are fictitious, I appreciate all who invest in my imagination by just being themselves.

CONTENTS

INTRODUCTION

S atisfaction guaranteed! Whether pleasing another or oneself, guarantee satisfaction. There are many things about life Oddiscy cannot control - sex was not one. Oddiscy grew up hearing of studies that said men think of sex far more than women do. Every seven seconds the man standing next to her in the store, at work, and even at church was thinking of sex. That small fact arouses her. Every seven seconds a man was thinking of sex, but it became impossible to count the frequency of which Oddiscy thought about men thinking of sex.

For Oddiscy, sex is more than pleasurable. Sex is not about love and horseback riding through fields filled with lilies on a sunny spring day. Sex must be erotic. Sex must be free. Sex must be full of imagination. The most crucial element of this art of sex is, was, and will always be the caress. She refers not to the touch, but to the caress of one's fingers and breath ever so lightly over the skin of another - on one's own skin. Oddiscy's escapades are never raunchy or crass. Satisfaction is guaranteed through sensuality, sophistication, sassiness, and uninhibited sexuality. Oddiscy has 3 rules: (1) Create boundaries, (2) Know your boundaries, (3) Insist other parties respect your boundaries. As time passed, her boundaries broadened. Her sensual imagination far exceeds any realistic physical possibilities. Sex must be unforgettable!

Much like the awareness of a man's near constant preoccupation with sex, Oddiscy became aware of the sensual elements of nature. She saw life as a ballroom filled with people, animals, celestial objects, atomic elements, space, time, naturally occurring formations, and more. She dances in that ballroom, switching partners from time to time. Oddiscy enjoys the dips. She looks forward to the falls. She lives for the passionate swings generating heated, sensual breezes.

Long ago, Oddiscy awakened to several sensual truths. Whether she plays cat-and-mouse with the Midnight Moon or relishes in the Kisses of a summer afternoon, Oddiscy enjoys the dance. Some partners left her humming a sultry tune called Lyrical Taboo. While others were supreme examples of Love's Portrayal. Unfortunately, in the midst of dancing, she at times finds herself reconciling pleasure and unfulfilled Desire. Like any sexy, long legged, curvy, brown-skinned beauty gliding on the dance floor well into the night, Oddiscy takes moments of rest. In the peace and quietness, she peeps into another ballroom
- other lives. In some of those rooms, she finds pain, loss, responsibility, holidays, fear, and tears. These moments empower her. Their truths invigorate her. Her passion for love translates into a passion for life. Oddiscy's sense of responsibility is awakened.

No one can tell Oddiscy's story. Only her words can speak to her wanting excitement. As she writes, she allows her mind and hands to wander. She thinks of each of her dance partners. Peppermint scent flows from her plump lips down through the pages of her journal as each breath inks the words. A very private person, Oddiscy refuses to reveal her issues with lust and desire. She feels no shame about the intensity of her rendezvous. Dance, bounce, twirl, sex was her playground. In the moment, she could be whomever she imagined herself - dominator, submissive, sensual, sexy, flamboyant, shy, impulsive, or withdrawn. Feather whips, leather tassels, and cold ice moving across her breast exist in her world of hidden excitement.

Oddiscy chooses a persona just as a woman would choose an outfit. She tours the closet of her psyche and picks one. Never giving all of herself to anyone but always giving the best of herself. She has no favorites among her conquests. Meticulous and practical, she chose carefully. "A satisfied man says nothing

because he wants to keep you all to himself. Satisfy him and he will keep your secrets," she says. Successful in the boardroom and the bedroom, Oddiscy dreamt of ways to please. Oddiscy believes, "It's not about the sex - It's about the touch. Touch a man just right, and he will release love all over you without ever entering you. A single kiss can touch a man's soul if you do it right. It's all about the touch. Master the touch, then upgrade to the caress!"

While she aims to please, she is not at all exclusively titled a giver. She expects the best and will not hesitate to stop a man if he delivers less than his best performance. He need not be stellar, or the best of the best, he needs to be his very best. She most definitely can tell the difference. Oddiscy gives for the joy of giving. You see, giving pleasure gives her pleasure. The more she pleases, the more she is pleased. So, Oddiscy is actually quite selfish. She pleases not for the lover, but for herself. She pleases so the other is compelled to return the favor. For if they want more, they must feed her insatiable appetite. The hardest part of any dance is making her the lover never learns of the reason for her passionate gifting. To this end, the lovers, given a promise of Satisfaction Guaranteed, soon realize Oddiscy can never be completely satisfied. The more a sex she gets, the more she wants. The more her body rises and falls, the more passionate she becomes. The wetter her lips, the more her lips desire. What is meant to satisfy her fills her with thirst and hunger. Oddiscy always wants more. Oddiscy always gets what she wants! Oddiscy always gives what she wants!

At times detached from her real feelings, she speaks as if her words, her desires, her lustfulness exists in a place far beyond herself. Maybe Oddiscy is too shy to admit she loses control. Maybe she refuses to accept her so-called sinful desires. Maybe the confessions are too real. Does Oddiscy really know Oddiscy best? Is she the best one to choreograph her dance moves? If not, who is? From where do the passions originate? Will they leave? Is it purity or filth? Romance or pornography? With ebony eyes, Oddiscy peers through the mirror into her own soul only to find more passion, more layers, and more unfulfilled desire.

Oddiscy has secrets. She is a secret. Those who know her wish they knew her. As sashes her six-foot frame through life, quite an unremarkable life, embracing the erotic energy in every facet of life. The old man standing in line to pump gas, she wonders if he still has sex and if so, how often. The teacher walking out of the school after a long day, removing her ponytail holder to reveal her hidden sensuality, Oddiscy imagines a lover awaiting her return home. Oddiscy sees the minister's wife proud of her husband's oratory abilities and envisions the passionate oral journey they must take on hot Sunday afternoons. Sunglasses are her signature. Oddiscy must hide her eyes. They are, after all, where her story is told. When someone, male or female, ventures a look into her eyes, they are drawn in. Spellbound, they wander aimlessly in the ebony ocean of her mind - awaiting her rescue. Will she take them into her world? One glance removes all sexual inhibitions. Erotic drunkenness. Who will sip off her wine?

"I reveal my curves, but not my flesh. I want them to dance with me. Too many women," she says, "chose to give away the flesh. They allow men, and women I guess, to imagine what sex would be like. They miss out on the most amazing and enticing aspect of the dance. They miss out on the moment when you look in the person's eyes, and they have no idea what to think. They are lost in a desire to taste the unknown. Foreplay begins with the mystery not the revelation." Oddiscy continues, "I love when they wonder what is underneath my suit. Sometimes, I challenge them greater by wearing a masculine tie with my pantsuit and stilettos - so many layers. They must imagine through so many layers." She takes a moment and smiles. It becomes obvious by the ever so light bouncing of her right leg over her left that she has journeyed off to a memory. Again, she speaks, "I relish in a simple 'Hello' which could very easily be

confused for an invitation to indulge in her sweet ribbon of chocolate - white chocolate. I do not send signals. I do not receive signals. I absorb energy. I relay pulses of energy."

In the pages that follow, Oddiscy expresses her sensual truths. She refused to revise her words. She resisted suggestions for editorial additions and subtractions. She wanted you to feel the purity of her energy. Oddiscy creates a beat, constructs a melody, and choreographs the dance. Dance with her...

MIDNIGHT MOON

OJust One Touch

ne evening while lying in bed, I looked at the time and then out the window. I saw a bright light that reminded me of the moonlight, but I knew it was not the Moon I wanted to see. At that moment, I realized that the Moon and I shared something special. At that special moment (slightly past midnight), I missed my Moon, its light, its *silhouette*, its boldness, its softness, and its distant display. My Moon reminds me to never forget that the sun shines and through the distance somewhere there exists closeness and warmth. I also realized that not just any Moon that could evoke these feelings -- it had to be the Midnight Moon. So, if I could talk to my Midnight Moon, I would say…

Hello Midnight Moon, can I talk to you?
Can I tell you all the things I'd like to do?
Will you promise to light my shadow?
And soften the moisture in my window?
Can I tell you the truth of my shyness
While you relieve my mouth of its dryness?
Can my privacy trust your secrecy?
As I tell you all about this fantasy?
Are you there Midnight Moon?
If you are not ready, then tell me it's too soon.
You see I have dreamed this before.
You and I across the floor.
Midnight Moon, you shine on desires I cannot
hide. In all fairness, I really tried.

But I need just one touch
Am I asking too much?

Hello Midnight Moon, can you feel my whisper?
My warm breath on your neck as the air grows crisper
Will you come as I call?
Will you rise as I fall?
Midnight Moon, I cannot see your hands
As my legs give way to spontaneous plans.
It's not always the timing and place
It's sometimes just the yearning for the embrace.
Under your beam I lie
Feeling your warmth on my thigh.
Can I tell you what's next and how we proceed?
You know it takes time to fulfill this need
Midnight Moon you slide in then you hesitate
Take it slow, don't worry, I'll wait
Now that you know, I need just one touch,
My question is…am I asking too much?

Hello, Midnight Moon, it's that time
I'm not going to make it difficult or make you read my mind
I want to touch you in places I cannot see
And let you know you can have any part of me.
Midnight Moon, I'm sorry, what did you say?
Yes, is the answer – Any part, any way?
Once you have me, I am yours
No one else will again take this
tour. It is your choice to climb or
ride.

Beneath you I maintain rhythm and stride.
To please you is my pleasure.
So, I ignore the forbidden and focus on the nectar.
Midnight Moon everything about me wants you here.
So now I pass the reigns, it's your turn to steer.
All I ask is for just one touch
Do you really think I'm asking too much?

The moment where chance, destiny, and fate collide with reality only happens under the Midnight Moon. Obeying reality, I know my Midnight Moon cannot and will not answer. But I still long for the chance to rest beneath me here - Midnight Moon there, and dream of how it would be if given the chance to have Just One Touch. Is it possible to miss the one you never met? Or, too long for a touch you never felt? My greatest fear is that my Midnight Moon will forever elude me. I so desire just one touch.

TLate Night Shadows

onight is like any other. She lay in her bed staring out the window, through the darkness, past the trees. Oddiscy saw her familiar Moon passing her window. Midnight Moon seemed different tonight. Usually big, bright, and overwhelmingly close, tonight he seemed pale, distant, and incomplete. Oddiscy tried to reach out, as she did so many times before, but tonight all she had were shadows – frightening shadows. The normally inviting Moon was now threatening. Oddiscy thought for a moment. Had she done something to result in this broadened expanse? Was the Moon still even there? What caused a retreat into the abyss?

With every thought, she became dizzy. With every moment that passed, she longed for a glimpse at her Moon. Oddiscy walked over to the window, lifted the resistant glass, and felt the misty breeze of the night air on her face. She longed for a touch. Her flesh was calling out for her Midnight Moon. She got nothing. I got nothing.

My heart reaches for places my hands could never touch
The yearning in my belly seems to be almost too much
Where can we meet and come out the shadows?
Or are you the one I will never know?
I sensed your touch and heard your voice
Yet I am left to reminisce on how your beam left me moist
My mouth calls to you
Hello Midnight Moon, can I talk to you?

Can I tell you all the things I'd like to do

I've made a simple wish and here's a clue
A night of endless love between me and you
(It's only your beam that distracts my view)
Hello Midnight Moon, let me show you more
Show you all the places I want to explore
One lonely kiss a silent lore
Midnight Moon, come, close the door
These are the things I'd like to say
At your distance, there is no way

Secrets of Midnight Moon

This is the space where there are no answers. Where love and hate are co-dependents of and to one another. This space, the only place that threatens the truth, is not to be shared with anyone but you. You may enter. Close the door behind you. Open your heart to me and close your mouth to the world. I trust you, if only for a minute. I chose not to trust anyone ever again. But there is something in your eyes. You heart hurts like mine. Your passion is activated by same lust as mine. Your soul serves the same God as mine. Because of this, all this, I trust you. I cannot say how long it will last. I cannot even say if it is still there with every word I write. But I can say at the birth of this thought you were the only man I trust. Maybe, it was that KISS.

Secrets of the Midnight Moon
Finally, the chance to see my Midnight Moon while the sun was shining
To look in its eyes and realize it too has a rising
Midnight Moon is not limited by time
It knows that it is only in a single moment a secret one can find
I speak of Midnight Moon as if it were the reality of my day
As if there were no limits to my time allotted to
play,
 I now know Midnight is the space in which it
shines

But it is the secret of the Moon I wish to find
I want to know the vastness of its beam
The quality of the stitching of its inseam
If its strength is limited by its smile
Or if its smile is limited by its trials
Midnight is the keeper of my Moon

Daylight is where its pleasures are
resumed, I had the chance to taste its
lips
To feel the pressures locked in its hips
But it was a secret daylight moment
A short division of time well spent
Midnight Moon owns more than it knows
With every word the passion grows
I look to the Sun now to light my way
To keep me until I again see my Moon in the day
I want more than a taste
Anything less than the chance to devour its passion is a waste
My Moon complicates the length of each leg
It keeps its words way too vague
To decode the secret requires another kiss
To get that kiss may require another secret wish
I do not fear where the Moon will lead
Now I know even under the shine of the Sun it can be freed
Are its arms as strong as they seem
Can I be pleased by the pulse of its beam?
Can I find a place in its rest?
Can its fingers tickle a tune on my breast?
Hold the light above the Moon
Once again, it may be too soon
It was not ready for its face to shine
Still blocked by the sun it wasn't the time
I try to hope and still believe
That my Moon's passion is mine to receive
I want my entrance to comply with the request of its exit
And its tongue to taste my sweet submit

I do not fear Moon's stolen words and stolen kiss

Nor its lips that located my secret wish

Moon took my denial and stole my fear

Subtracted my passion from my lust leaving me with a single tear

I cannot overexcite myself

I return passion to its proper place on the shelf

Until it is safe

Midnight Moon can again return to its secret place

Hidden Moon

When I envision my Midnight Moon
It is you, I picture – finely groomed
The face I will never forget
Is that same face I have never met
I look deep in the eyes of every man I pass or meet
They only remind me that it is you I seek
There is no other one
I fear my search has only just begun
My heart beats for the day I hear your voice
I know, even today, you are my only choice

Midnight Moon, I long for your touch
Knowing the embrace will be overwhelming – nearing too much
Love unrelated to status or stature
Physique and society are no match for our nature
I am completely incomplete as I wait
From my perfectly imperfect imagination to image will one day translate
You are sexy to me in a way I have yet to see
Although I have never seen you so I must trust what my body tells me

Searching for Midnight Moon!

I cannot see you from where I am
My eyes search from every window they can
But it is obvious you are not there - or here
Unlike the sun, you offer no warmth to comfort me when the clouds overtake the skies
You fail to share even the modest light a shy sun supplies
I want to feel you and know you are there - anywhere

Midnight Moon, you have never failed me until now
A seductive breeze through my window, ajar, leaves my legs crossed and my tears bound
I looked, but it is obvious you are not there - or here
I opened to you, releasing every secret desire
In return, I lay wondering whether false hope is all that will transpire
Yet I need to feel you and know you are there - anywhere

My eyes search every level of the atmosphere
My heart grows closer and farther from fear
It's increasingly obvious, to my eyes and heart, you are not there – or here
I revealed all I am, possibly, too soon or too much or for the wrong reason all together
Expecting reciprocated knowledge incapable of weighing down a feather

But, still, I desire to feel you and know you are there – anywhere

My fingers trace the seams of the night sky - defenseless

Each ridge tickles my senses reminding me of the nights your tickle aroused my senses
To my senses it becomes obvious you are not there – or here
I showed you the original designs of my flesh
Receiving alterations to my souls was the price I paid to for us to mesh
Pulling within is the yearning to feel you and know you are there – anywhere

My feet want to retrace my steps to the place I last saw you
Each toe a different memory, making me mistrust the view
There is no denying, it's obvious you are not there – or here
Looking back at all I gave, there is not a single moment of sensual creativity I regret
I got nothing I needed while getting what I never knew I wanted – no regret
I cannot help but to want to feel you and know you are there – here – anywhere!

The Voice of the Midnight Moon (This is Between Me and You)

I n his voice, I could hear his future. With every faint exhale, I could feel his past. I seemed to know him the moment I saw his silhouette. Not my type or the time carved image of my future, his presence overtook me. It was a late, hot, summer night dinner party. Arriving alone, I was the odd number. This was a rare moment of confidence. This night, I felt single, not alone.

A simple chain restaurant with a uniquely charming atmosphere, the marbled floors married perfectly with my patent-leather black and red stilettos with metallic silver heels. The lighting was warm and romantic. As I held steadily to the polished mahogany rail on the steep curving staircase, I held my head up and back straight. At the bottom of the never-ending staircase, I stood at the quaint bar awaiting direction to the proper table. I looked over my shoulder. There HE stood. Startled by his striking appearance, I muttered a childish insult. Thus began the dance.

His laughter from across the table seemed to take a seat next to me. I asked question after question, not to know more about him, but to hear his voice. His voice commanded my respect. He was not much taller than average, but his demeanor presented him as an imposing eight feet tall. The candle on the table flickered, as did my heart. The band played a tune to which my body yearned to sway. The aroma of delectable food played on my tongue as I wondered about his velvety feel of his tongue entangled with mine. Checking to see if his date was aware, I kept a balance between professional and playful. As I once did with a middle school crush, I played a game that pulled him close then pushed him just as far away. All I was told of him before that night was obviously wrong.

His date, my friend, narrated stories of laziness, inability, weakness, and brokenness. His eyes told quite a different story. His mannerisms could not hide his strength and manliness. I was scared. I was lost in his voice.

New territory. New chapter. New appeal. This was my secret. I could never reveal to anyone how much (and how quickly) my heart longed for him. Suddenly, I felt inadequate. With every sip of wine, I spoke more directly providing hints of my previously quieted hope. With every sip of his beer, his voice deepened. My friend, his date, seemingly unaware, only added to my uneasiness. Hands tucked away, I played with the eggshell-colored tablecloth, careful not to upset the emptying stemware, hoping the night would soon end simultaneously praying it would never. I wanted to tell him my hopes and dreams. He had to know my future. The band continued to play. The pinot noir swirled in the glass as the waiter slowly poured using the opportunity to glance down at my glistening breasts. Could the waiter sense my excitement rising and hips shifting in my chair as drop after drop after pounding drop of wine created a tiny sea of lust in my glass?

My mind tussled with the image of him, the guy, my friend's guy, stealing quick glances of the edges of my dress clinging to the form of my breast. What about my past? The attentive waiter asked if the table wanted anything else. Noticing my pulse quickening, my breathing stopped for the briefest moment – an involuntary moment of silence. I wanted to shout, "Yes, I want him – TO GO!" Instead, I spoke for the table releasing the waiter to attend to other customers. My attention momentarily split, an envisioned the tip –the tip I would give the waiter if he ushered me into the backroom. The waiter could most certainly satisfy the immediate rise of passion. His broad chest and tattooed arms screamed for release. I could almost hear the blood flowing through the bulging veins in his arms. My eyes wandered below his belt slyly investigating his prominence. Silently, I questioned his thickness. Licking my lips is wanton desire, I snapped back to reality, I caught myself just before the moan escaped.

As the conversations grew more intense and the sound of forks hitting plates filled the air, I retreated into the deepest part of her mind…

"Friendship chains clanging loudly
Overwhelming the sound of my heart's pounding
Loyalty, duty, sisterhood, linked together
Threatened what was once thought as never

The question of love is unrealistic
The question of friendship is far too simplistic
Thriving on the wondrous intrigue
My heart's love is strengthened through friendship fatigue"

Who is to say what should happen? I knew after tonight I had nothing to fear. Everything I felt, every sensual contemplation would mean nothing. All I would have is this mysterious moment. Calmness descended as my spoon broke through the glassy top of the passion fruit vanilla crème brûlée'. The champagne congratulated my ability to resist, not the guest of honor as intended. Its bubbles applauded me for not being vocal in my attraction (as was my usual style). I did what was right – this time. Rather, I did which was correct. I sat, squirming a bit in my armchair, feeling wronged. I felt cheated. My loyalty to my friend remained intact. I navigated the whole evening trying not to say his name. To say his name would make his image permanent. To say his name may give away my sultriness. He had to stay just some guy that …that guy that…that stole my heart.

The drive home was quiet. I did not want his voice to fade. I hung on to his every word wanting my legs to hang around his neck as he pulled himself deeper into my world. My mind replayed his every word. No music. Windows up. Only the hum of the car in the background existed. Overdrive.

"Waiting to be loved in a new way
Searching for the one man willing to stay"

His voice boomed in my head as if he were next to me. My thoughts left the white lined highway…

"Longing for someone worthy of my embrace
Somewhere in love I will find my place."

When I arrived home, I laid partially clothed across my bed gazing at the Moon. I still refused to mouth his name. In my thoughts, I could not stop repeating his name, hearing it in his own voice, over and over. The Moon captivated me, just as he did. Hand gliding near my heart, legs misty from the summer heat, I closed my eyes…

"Your look has a special touch
Your presence caresses me
Something about your smile is almost too much
Could we find the space beyond ecstasy?
This is between you and me

I stepped into you face
Expecting to turn you away
Instead, I clinch my fist and my lips find their place

With my eyes closed, I attempt to say
This is between me and you

Secrets kill and secrets give life
No words can give justice to what we could share
Silence consented to our secret tonight
Love suffocates on anticipation in the air
This is between you and me"

The phone rings. My eyes popped open… "Just making sure you got home alright." His voice visited for a moment. Struggling to answer, I simply said, "Yes." A smile formed across my face rivaled in size only by the universe. He spoke several more words. I tendered many more responses. Preoccupied, I cannot recall any of the actual words he and I exchanged. With each word he spoke, I wanted more. After "Good-bye," I turned off the light, smiled, and closed her eyes…

"Clothes on the bed
Feet on the floor
Nothing to be said
Do not disturb on the door
This is between me and you

Hands locked
Legs open
Someone's on top
Concentration unbroken
This is between you and me

Cool heat
Moaning smile
Empty treat
Single file
This is between me and you"

Dream fading, I whispered his name. "This is between you and me." That night
he became the voice of the Midnight Moon.

The Rise and Fall of the Midnight Moon

Unbearable attraction
Unfulfilled passion
Unspeakable tension
Immeasurable emotion

Midnight Moon, here I am wanting
Heart pounding, legs shaking
Ready for your arrival
I dreamed of this moment, this day
My visions venture past passion to erotic denial
Finally so much to do and so little to say

Shine all over me, leaving your glow
Rise and fall on me, above and below
This is the time to take me where you please
This is the place to make all things happen
I lay on my back with my mind at ease
Then comes the flood of clear liquid satin

Unbearable attraction
Unfulfilled passion
Unspeakable tension

Immeasurable emotion

Midnight Moon, I can think of no one else

You are the only one with the power to ring my bells
I long for the long of you
I am tempted by your enticement
I want for the want of you
I am in full surrender within your vice grip

I am locked into this…
Unbearable attraction
Unfulfilled passion
Unspeakable tension
Immeasurable emotion

Midnight Moon, it is you!

The Night My Midnight Moon Disappeared

Hands pressed against the window
She opens her eyes intently
She gazes out at the missing glow
Her Midnight Moon now her enemy

Midnight Moon left with no warning
Left her standing disillusioned by the absence
She loses control of her fingers, tracing
Her breath warming the cold glass, essence

Like every other Moon before
Like every glow she ever felt
Midnight Moon escaped through some secret door
Crushed by the silence, she knelt

Feeling the shiver of her hands
Wanting the warm of his touch
She rolled to one side in an attempt to stand
Standing was just a bit too much

One tear, two tears, then many more
One moan, two moans, then she sobbed.
Overwhelmed by her lonely core,
Onward to the darkness her cooling heart throbbed

She stops to wonder, "What will come of the day"?
If the Midnight Moon was merely resting?
When he appeared, what would he say?
He said nothing, nothing worth trusting!

He was gone,
Midnight Moon, and every hope in him.
It was all gone!
She laughed as if it would be her last sin.

She gazed one last time at the night sky.
One last hope in what could have never been.
The last act of an endlessly flawed performance, cry!
She closed her eyes hoping to see Midnight Moon in her dreams again!

Unannounced Arrival of Midnight Moon

Oddiscy thought Midnight Moon was forever gone. She just knew continued hoping on his arrival was an exercise in improbability. Then, one day, there was a knock. Unprepared, without a clue to spark expectation, Oddiscy ran to the door. Thinking:

I am hesitant to open the door.
Even, to take a one-eyed glimpse through the peephole.
The possibility of you as my future scares me.
The possibility of you as my past scares me more.

There are no certainties in life and even less in love
There is no forever unless the love is infinite
Is love infinite?
Is forever in our future?

Could it be that Midnight Moon has revealed himself in the light?
Could Midnight Moon be closer than he once appeared?
I thought we reached our conclusion.
I thought the possibility of you faded wholly into fantastic memory

Midnight Moon, the earthquakes as your presence shifts my atmosphere
My breath gallops away on a panther's back as it realizes its strength
My passion explodes from the molten river in my heart, creating and recreating
as it grows
There is no time for time

My heartbeat is not a measure of life, but of the intensity of my longing.
My breasts imprison the thumping away, pulsating, vibrating aftershocks of
wanting.
How does one request more of what one has never experienced?
How does a mountain remember the steps of unexplored exploration?

I remembered your smile when at first, I saw it.
I remembered your strength without even feeling it.
I remembered your wisdom before you spoke a singular word.
I remember, I recall, I re-envision every measured increment of you.

Midnight Moon, frightened, I find myself traveling toward an inescapable vortex.
I stand behind the door, listening to the knock, wondering.
Is this my imagination creating another hope of you?
Or, is my hope of your blinding the reality of you?

In this moment, I hold the doorknob of my heart.
I shed the delicate layers of my imagination
I stand in the pools of growing passions.
I pull open the door exposing your imagined form.

The One and Only, Midnight Moon Returns

Once again, the Midnight Moon has descended. He looked in the window. He knocked on the door. I opened.

In all your fullness, I bathe in your light
Your beam once again extends over my being
I fall deeper for your rise to limitless heights
Caught in your crippling glance my legs are freeing
The need cycles through my veins
The fire causes my thighs to tremble
The intensity rules my moistening domain
My tongue stutters out meaningless syllables

Midnight Moon, I yearn for your power
Pulsating, vibrating, immensely overwhelming power
I feel the impression of your supporting tower
I grab hold of the moment and hunger to devour
As you lean slowly forward into my window,
I should tell you exactly what I want
Afraid of what may come my words linger in limbo

Then you pull back as some cruel sexy taunt

There is only one Moon in my midnight
Only one beam that will penetrate my window's pane
Only one shadow that will suppress my light
From all others, I choose to refrain

Midnight Moon, my heart beats for you
The moments retreat for you
The cycle of life waits for you
There is only one as extreme as you!

To you I reveal my inner most secret places
Giving you freedom to create and recreate as you please
In the morning, you leave without the faintest trace
Only to return the next night with the impact of a cold spring breeze
My skin tingles as it awakens
My taste buds rise on my tongue
My middle back arches revealing the fruit to be taken
Midnight Moon, never question, you are the one!

No one man, to date, can permanently claim the title "Midnight Moon." The Moon has many faces and phases. With each comes an experience, a lesson, and a unique memorable pleasure. My eyes, heart, and legs reach out in search of the next Midnight Moon who will reveal aspects of his persona never before known. Daringly, I continue to seek. Intently, I will find.

KISSES

One moment
One hug
One smile
One kiss

A Kiss

These were her moments between work and home. The moments she normally spent reflecting on her day, and decompressing from the pressures inherent in the world of business meetings, calls with attorneys, arguing with accountants, and proving that a woman, this woman, can do the job of any man in the business. Her leg shook against the steering wheel. Her lips quivered at the thought of him. The tension in the office made her yearning almost unbearable. She thought he had forgotten her. She thought she had forgotten him. But today, the flowers came.

The card read:
"I'm in town on business. If you are interested in meeting up, call me. Unforgettably Yours, Darren."

A repressed memory, the long drive home without traffic opened her mind to that afternoon lingering in an empty corner office looking out on the Philadelphia skyline. As she stood planning the chest moves necessary to ensure her name is stenciled on the glass office door, he walked in. Hand on her shoulder, he told her how he thought she was terrific and intelligent. Paying him little attention, she dreamt of picking out office furniture, and sending emails announcing the merger and her promotion. "It could happen any day," she thought.

The Greek-god-like specimen of a man dressed in a three-piece navy blue custom-tailored fine pin-striped suit with a fitted ivory shirt and manly fuchsia tie gently tapped her shoulder. His cologne caressing the tip of her nose, startled, she turned. "How long was he standing there? I thought he'd gone." Oddiscy recalled his cufflinks sparkling in the sun. Just then, she realized, her hand was tucked between the buttons of her unforgiving satin blouse. So emerged in thought, she had begun gently massaging her breast as she stood in the office window. He tapped her just as her middle finger reached her perky nipple. "I just arrived," he assured her. "Please don't stop on my account." She smiled. Clearing her throat, she stretched out her hand, "Oddiscy." He kissed her hand, the hand that was on her breast, and with a booming voice that vibrated through her, "Darren." They walked away.. After a meeting where she learned he was her new client, they found themselves in a secluded area of the floor. Darren invited her for a brief cocktail and a bite to eat to celebrate the new association.

The phone rings. "Hello," he says as if annoyed by the intrusion. "I am not available this evening…I'm sure it can wait until morning…. Yes, I know. Yes." He kept talking. All Oddiscy could focus on was his full lips repeating "Yes." Darren turns to her, checks his watch, and slowly raises his hand to her chin so as not to alarm her. Almost instinctively, Oddiscy raised her chin and closed her eyes. His lips felt like home. His tongue filled her mouth. Darren's breath tasted a creative mix cinnamon and peppermint. Oddiscy could not separate her breath from his. The kiss only lasted a few seconds but felt like an eternity. "I apologize. I must resend my invitation. Something has come up. When do you leave?" She replied, still lost in the moment, "I…I leave tonight." Well, lovely lady, I'll be in Boston in early October. If you find yourself in Philly before then, please look me up. If not, I will call you when I am in your neck of the woods."

The mere mention of the word "neck" quickened her pulse. "Sounds like a plan." With the graceful turn of a ballet dancer, Oddiscy left him behind. Each step made her aware of how long it had been since she felt the touch of a man. As each leg rose and fell creating an inviting prance, she could feel the wetness absorbed by her panties.

The screaming of a car horn on the opposite side of the highway divider snatched Oddiscy back to reality. The window was cracked allowing the breeze of the autumn night to brush against her cheek. There still had been no one since her brief encounter with Darren. The new position at work distracted her from exploring and physical positions with a man. She remained appeased by the pleasure toys in her purse, car armrest, by her bed, in her desk at work, and even hidden in her Bible bag disguised as a bookmark. This had to end. Before she realized…

She quietly said, "*I want a kiss*"

A kiss that tells me I am the best part of his day
A kiss that says more than any amount of words could ever say
The deepest of kisses with the longest of holds
The kiss that reveals all the stories untold

She thought, "I want a kiss"

The kind of kiss that ignores the world
The kind of kiss as simple as boy meets girl
A kiss that forgets the pains of the past
A kiss that tells me that forever will last

I want a kiss
That special kiss
That - can't wait 'til the next kiss kiss

Hmmm…I want a kiss

She tried not to say, "I want a kiss"

A kiss that walks me through a smile
A kiss that brings me back from denial
The strongest of kisses with the gentlest embrace
The kiss that knows not time nor place

Oddiscy tried to drive. She tried to concentrate. But - the wind. She pulled along the side of the road, looked in the mirror…

Her eyes said, "I want a kiss"

The kind of kiss that was born from affection The kind of kiss that forces reflection
A kiss that inspires the hope of more A kiss that lifts my feet off the floor

I want a kiss
That love long kiss
That –this better not be the last kiss kiss

Yeah…I want a kiss

Her lips said it best, "I want a kiss"

A kiss that entices exposure of my secret wish

A kiss that leaves me speaking French Spanish and English The sexiest of kisses from the smoothest tongue
The kiss that says I'm the one

Her heart said it more, "I want a kiss"

The kind of kiss that never walks away The kind of kiss that only stops to play A kiss that has the power to please
A kiss that requires release

Oddiscy runs in her suede purple pumps and flaring winter white trench coat to his door. She looks at the floor. In an irrational moment, a speck of a second, she found herself...

With no "Hello" Grabbing his face... Pulling him close...

She whispered, "I want a kiss"
That dangerous kiss
That "I'm gonna leave your lips tingling from the kiss" kiss That special kiss
That "I can't wait 'til the next kiss" kiss That love long kiss
That "I know this better not be the last kiss" kiss

So...Can I get a kiss?

The door closed!

It Was Just a Kiss

Waiting through the fire
Finally the apex of my desire
Overtaken by the thought of you
Fingers go places I want you to
But they can only calm not fulfill
It is you I want to feel
You I want between my legs
You I want to ask me to beg
Your name I want to call when I come
There is a voice I want to hear – only one
My nipples tingle when I recall our kiss
My wetness acknowledges a passion I cannot dismiss
The look in your eyes told me I wanted you
The slip of your tongue told me you wanted me too
It is I alone tonight
Me saying this isn't right
This is not how it is supposed to be
I should not be the one pleasing me
I should have your hands grabbing my thighs
You making me come forcing pleasured cries
Oh for the chance to please you entirely
The chance to kiss your body
To feel your manhood between my lips
To have my thirst satisfied with just one sip
There is juice, and there is nectar

But my desire tells me you have something better
I am ready for the long awaited
For the language that cannot be translated
The language that can only be spoken during the height of passion
The voice that cannot be released by any form of masturbation
I am ready to feel IT
To feel its pulse realize the perfect fit
To be pushed past the limit of satisfaction
Past elation
Past joy
Past me being your toy
Past the point of being able to relax
Past the point of climax
Delivered to the exact moment of "There is nothing better"
So wet I can only get wetter
So hot, I can only get hotter
So deep, you can only get deeper
That is where I want us to arrive
You see you move like you have a stride
Like you have a hidden secret
I will find it whether I have to swallow or spit
I will find what makes you want more
I will find what move, kiss, spot, or lick is your ultimate lure
This I promise
Whatever you wish - I promise
I have waited for this for so long
No need for flowers or a love song
Just nakedness
But for now, I am limited to the thought of the kiss

The one that started all this
It was just a kiss

LYRICAL TABOO

Play the music so I can be transported
All my negativity collected then aborted
My life in the control of every note
Gently coast on a sea of newfound hope

*S*ome people hum a tune, turn up the radio, pop in a favorite CD, or shuffle songs - I like men that create music. It could be live music or not. I only have a small radio in my loft. My music collection is limited. But, I am a music lover. I am a lover of music. I love music. Music loves me. Music caresses me. Music makers inspire me. With each musical relationship, I had but one request…

> Play the music so I can be transported
> All my negativity collected then aborted
> My life in the control of every note
> Gently coasting on a sea of newfound hope

Sounds like a little too much. Yeah, I know, it is. There is something spectacular about a man that is musically talented. He has a passion about him. He understands the relationship between body, mind, spirit, and soul. He is gifted with the ability to create a bridge between all four parts of our humanity. So, I submit to the musicians of the world the music of my heart and sounds of my soul.

All That Is Taboo

Singing the song of my love for you
The melody of all that is taboo
I lay in my bed
Hands on my head
Trying to imagine you there
Aware that everything I feel is taboo

That everything that I want about you
Is wrong to do
I can see it front to rear
It all seems so clear
All that stand between this and reality is fear
Your arms around my waist
My hand stroking the side of your face

Singing the song of my love for you
The melody of all that is taboo
Just before we discover that we are each other's secret place
I would love just one taste
Just one chance to know
But I lay here
Trying to block the rivers flow

Singing the song of my love for you
The melody of all that is taboo
Oppressed by thoughts of "no" and "go"
I want you beside me
To find me
To allow your manhood to hide in me
I want to see
I want to make you happy

Eyes opening
Wondering
Longing
Wanting

Willing
Singing

Singing the song of my love for you
The melody of all that is taboo
As my eyes begin to open wide
I must admit I must decide
Whether to go on love's free ride
Some say just go with the tide
But it feels way too strong
I may find out where I am is where I belong

So I lay in my bed
Hands on my head
Feeding the passion unfed
Never dead
My love has saved a place for you
Humming the melody of all that is taboo

Singing the song of my love for you
The melody of all that is taboo

Taboo or not, music makes me smile. Sometimes I could not separate the smile
gifted from the music from the smile given by the man. This particular music
man truly made me smile. The thought of him, his music, and his hands playing
music made me smile. Like any drug, the high was temporary. The smile never
lasted more than a day. I had to see him again. I had to get another dose of
what gave me the smile. He and I were not about sex it was about connecting.

Sex was a product of the musical connection. Music was the foreplay. Tunes created the sensation of thousands of tiny fingers massaging me ever so softly - vibrations. I smiled. The smiles faded. I smiled again. He sang in my ear. I smiled. He laughed at his mistakes. I smiled. When it was over, and he faded into the background of my life, I still smile. There was one smile that fragmented my heart. Not every smile is meant to be forever. But, some smiles I wish I never experienced. Better to have loved…better to have smiled I guess.

One-Day Smile

My friends keep telling me not to catch feelings
To remember you and me have no serious dealings
I know they are right, but when you leave
Oh, Baby when you leave
The feeling I have I will not admit
The feelings I have I cannot believe
I know I'm not in love, but I know I love being with you
When we apart, I cannot stop smiling and reminiscing about time we had
But the next day, not a word from you, leaves me feeling sad
Wanting you back
Wanting you back here where I am at
When will this end
Or when will we begin
Yeah it is like that
Perfect for me
Loving your body
Especially inside me

You give me a one-day smile
That seems like it will never fade
You give me a one-day smile
I wish you had stayed
Baby you give me a one day smile
An inside out, all day, real live smile

I try to ignore the truth
And blame it on my youth

I try to accept this and say it is what I need
Why do I want to be tied down when I fought so hard to be freed
So what, I never smiled like this before
Life is full of paths
And this is just another door
Happiness is a choice, not a given decision
But you made me smile
You do not know what that means
You painted a smile that can outshine sun beams

You give me a one-day smile
That seems like it will never fade
You give me a one-day smile
I wish you had stayed
Baby you give me a one day smile
An inside out, all day, real live smile

After walking alone so long
I need a pretty song
A theme that will make me dance, groove, moonwalk, and slide
Baby a theme to match the smile I cannot hide
I am mature enough to know this is not forever
But for now it's whenever, whatever, however
See I feel what you are doing and how it's done
I need to be fulfilled
And your today's chosen one
Whether this will last for an inch or a mile
Music maker thanks for the smile
You give me a one-day smile

That seems like it will never fade
You give me a one-day smile
I wish you had stayed
Baby you give me a one day smile
An inside out, all day, real live smile

Rain dance

The best part of music is the dance. The soul dances. The eyes dance. The feet follow. Music when connected to the right words fall on you – rains down on you. You can feel it tapping through the layers of your skin, adjusting the rhythm of you heart, and finally, it speaks to your soul. You can see the notes linger in the air. So, you dance. I dance. I dance even between the raindrops. I dance in the puddles of time. I spin with power and intensity of a hurricane. I put my hands up and twirl in the whirlwind of the notes. I dance. You dance. We dance the Rain Dance.

Rain falling on my skin
Sprinkle from above
Covering me with kisses of love
Lost in a timeless vision
Wasting time wishing
There was a lover
To drown out the thunder
Bodies colliding
The release from tension to orgasm subsiding.

The rain
No longer a symbol of pain
But of promises hiding
Dreaming
The thunderous boom
Headboard hitting the wall of your room
I can feel the rain falling
Between my legs showering
Rinsing
Making my skin more sensitive to the love we make
Clearing the last impression made
Rain never go away
Stay with us the entire day
My skin needs the embrace
My mind needs the clarity
Our hearts need sincerity.
Problems disappear
As you grab me from the rear
Spinning me past the point where pleasure is born from fear
I sense the thunder, but you hear you whisper, "I'm here."
Each raindrop covers me, one by one single tear.
I feel the rain, I sense your strength.
Powerful, somehow, we are floating -
drenched My lips you kissed then devour.
It is our sweet hour
To do the rain dance
Confirming our meeting was not change
Feeling of rain enhanced
So we danced

Save every dance for me to enjoy
Allow me to smile like a woman with a new toy
Feeling free from the usual sneaky ploys
I am your girl, you are my boy
Feel the rain refresh.
Take your time, do not rush.
It is my turn to taste your flash.
My turn to control how are our bodies meld and mesh
I will show you how to understand the rain
Thunder, the lightning, there is no shame
No one around
By the usual rules, we are not bound
I will explore places in pleasure no woman before has found.
Feel the rain-enjoy the chance
All that is left- our naked prance
Our Sweet Rain Dance

Unsung Melody

There is a tune my heart is humming
Beneath all the pain and moaning
It hums of a love it has never known.
It hits notes happiness has never shown.
The tune of love is vibrating.
So unfamiliar, it keeps resonating.
This song has no words unto which to hide its tune.
There is only the melody and the midnight Moon
It ushers me from scene to scene and task to task
It swirls beneath my smiling mask.
It is my soundtrack to a movie never made.
It is the lead drummer in an imaginary parade
I can hear the music loud and strong.
When I'm near you I know it's not wrong
You make the melody.
You are the melody.
In your baseline, I find normality.
In your silence, I understand formality
I tried to hum the tune aloud
Only you can introduce it to the crowd.
Only you could turn this melody into reality.
Only you can transform silence into loves fatality.
You are my unsung love song.
The hum for which I long.
There in your arms I find my crescendo.

Pure, free of innuendos
Accepting the dissonance
As unexpected recompense.
I hum.
I hum in my heart so loud.
Wondering if it's wrong to be proud.
I look for you.
Can't find you.
But my heart hums.
I hum.
No, you are the words I swallow cowardly.
Rehearsing the tune of my heart's unsung melody

Melody, tune, tone, notes, keys, chords, and stroke are a few of the ingredients that make up the theme song to the rain drops of my life. When walking between the raindrops you have to be aware of timing. What best to help maintain timing that music. It counts for you. It pauses for you. It tells you when to speed up or slow down. Music makes you yield to it rather than yield for it. I am grateful for the gift of music, and for the men (and women) that make it. With ever raindrop that falls and ever note that rises, I can live through it all.

Just a thought: The rhythm of sex is different from that of love. It can at times be difficult to tell one from the other. Denial can be useful in such cases. I can just pretend I hear love when I am really dancing to the rhythm of lust. I do not often confuse sex for love, but I do confuse love for sex. He is in love, and I am in it for the sex. Hey, it happens. Why is taboo for a woman, a lady, a sexually confident lady, to admit that sex is all she wants?

I mean companionship is great, but life can get too complicated at times. Sometimes, I am just too busy to cater to every need of a man. When I am in a relationship, I am all in! I want to please and pleasure a man in every way and in every area of our lives. I mean, I do not go overboard. Also, I do have certain expectations of reciprocated efforts. But there are times that I just do not have the emotional energy to share. Corporate life demands so much of my time and attention. My sex life can become more about thrilling release than an emotional merger or acquisition. Maybe it is just me. Maybe I am being too honest. Maybe Oddiscy is just a sexually frustrated workaholic. I joke. I, Oddiscy, am in love with sex. I know when to say when. I am not a sex addict. Or, am I?

I simply appreciate the human form. From time to time, a man enters my life that excites me in ways I could never anticipate. The sex becomes secondary. A close second, but second, nonetheless. Primarily, he becomes my muse. It is almost as if he reveals a new layer of me that I did not know exist. I remember one such guy. His skin was so smooth, masculine, but smooth. His face was a rich chocolate mocha complexion underlying a well-groomed goatee. This chiseled specimen in his mid-thirties was so sensitive and understanding. He seemed to want to please me as much as I wanted to please him. In fact, he often refused my advances as I began at his lips, kissed his chin, slowly licked then blew on his chest, and slowly traveled toward his pulsating penis. He would quickly grab my arms, flip me over, and lick-kiss-slurp me until his face shined with my slippery glaze. He was my muse!

aMUSEment

If you only knew how I feel about you
How I long for you
How I thirst for you
If you only knew that my heart has no rhythm without your beat
Life, liberty, and the pursuit of ecstasy
Chasing orgasms surpassing love
Sitting side by side awaiting destiny
Dreaming of the right one to come right now
If you only knew
Until then, you are for my aMUSEment

If you only knew that my body secretly arches when you enter the room
How my mind creates sensual scenarios
How my dreams realign themselves in hopes of joining you
If you only knew that I wish for your love more than I wish for riches
Synchronized breathing tells its own tale
Quick glazed glances of bitter denial
Let the souring odor of friendship prevail?
Never! Alternate the reality as you are my "he" and I your "she"
If you only knew
Until then, you are for my aMUSEment

If you only knew that my arms feel empty until we hug
How my hands become restless in your absence
How my tongue finds no relief

If you only knew that I admire the indecent decency of your form
Awakened, moist, thirsty, I feel for you
My hand reaches slow and to find the place you left vacant
A sensuality only comparative to tiny feather floating on a summer morning dew
My mouth, wide and receptive, poised as if created for you
If you only knew
Until then, you are for my aMUSEment

If you only knew that I see a future in your eyes
How the hope in your arms excites me
How the love in your words leaves my hungry
If you only knew that I admire you
Only your faith can quash my fears
Only your persistence can overtake my procrastination
Only your "you" can better my "me"
Only your Adam could satisfy my
Eve If you only knew
Until then, you are for my aMUSEment!

My Key – My Girl

> *Oddiscy took a moment, hand gently covering her eyes, to reminisce. She allowed her thoughts to tumble back to a time before she knew the alleged wrongness of what felt right. Her first kiss was the key. Caressing her thigh, she felt a tingle much like the first time. She wondered, "Maybe there are things only a girl can know about a girl. Maybe I should have ... But I love ... it felt so good then." It unlocked all sensuality she would ever know. In that moment, Oddiscy was on a quest back to her first love and irrational desire – girl to girl. It was a brief memorial tour summarizing years of back and forth lust and denied pleasure. Jealousy. Passion. Desire. Intimacy. Purity.*

A new way to look at you
The girl I forgot I ever knew
Looking at youth be true
A sea of memories to sail through

You are the girl I first loved
Not clear on the challenge of above
Your eyes told a story, my peaceful dove
Your lips kiss glory out of its glove

I walk to you forgotten girl
In my dreams, you create my freeing world
I'll never forgot the silhouette swirl
Hand to hand a girl's first pearl

I will never forget you, my Key!

Key was the key to it all. She was Oddiscy's first. She was the one all other lovers would have to measure up to. Key was the one that got away. Over the years, Oddiscy looked at other women, curious about their pleasure spots and form, but there never was a true attraction. Key was the only one who ever brought about such uncontrollable emotions in Oddiscy, male or female. Once in a while, late at night, when the Midnight Moon has drifted off to sleep or faded away, Oddiscy's hand ventures under the sheets, thinking of Key, remembering her touch. It was not meant to be. No regrets, Oddiscy still wishes she could tell Key what she meant to her. Not all love is understandable. Not all love is logical. Not all love can be classified. But, love is love, passion is passion, even if it must be kept a kept a secret locked away in the past. Sometimes, once is enough.

DESIRE

Anyone can give me sex
But it takes a special man to give me pleasure
A certain man to release my stress
A different man to love and treasure

Something in me, Something in you

I have waited so long for the silence to be quieted. I have waited for the loud, thunderous sound of peace to subside. Yet it is here.

Something in me wants something in you
For your voice to answer some unknown call
For your fingers to trace some absent pattern in my heart
I sit waiting and wondering what I want or if I want anything at all

I want you to want something from me
I want permission to fulfill a need that no one else can
be there for you – trusting you
I want always to be the one stoking your hand

My thoughts know your voice too well
Reminding me that you are not what I fear
Your love is the destination of my quieted travels
Hope refusing to drown in the chorus of clapping tears

What a Woman Wants

I want you to…
Lick me in places only fingers can reach
Taste the juices that drip from my peach
Nibble my nipples just a bit
Get on your knees and head down while I sit

I want you to…
Walk around naked without any shame
Finger love me until I go insane
Hold me down and love me slow
Sex me like your putting on a show

I want you to…
Treat me like we're in love
Smack my bottom soft with a leather glove
Use an ice cube to awaken my flesh
Lick the honey off my breast

I want you to…
Call me names that make me feel special
Make me holler things that sound spiritual
Take my mind places I've never been
Do a few things your mama said was a sin

I want you to…

Let me ride you like a wild bull
Cum until every part of me is full
Share with me lasting orgasms
Not stopping until every muscle spasms

I want you to...Love me
I want you to...Sex me
I want you to...Caress me
I want you to...Cum with me

Saturday Night Fever

In search of satisfaction
A chance at soul relaxation
Peace and cosmic relation
Just a foot into a new situation
Destroying the old creation
Where I was and can no longer be
Placed in a position where I can see
And focus on what is to be me
What is to be us
What will be togetherness
My mind and soul themselves caress
Releasing what I need to confess
Unknown stress
Enhanced by the desire to undress
Life and see it in its nakedness
Its fullness
Its realness
Its excitement
Forgiving the things seeded with resentment
Feeling things deeper than sentiment
Smiling while my heart and breath lament
At last my chance - my accent
My glance at higher ground
To lose myself and yet be found
Within myself looking around

Joy and pain simultaneously resound
There is not volume controlled
No reigns on me to hold
It is all so simple to unfold
I have other lives I need to mold
Hidden stories that must be told I need to speak
And allow my essence to leak
Cursing visions of what is sad and bleak
Mistaking the seemingly meek
For who is really the bona fide weak
Yet suave and sleek
Back erect
Too tired to reflect
A path I must select
I have to blow the battle horn
I have to swing the battle ax
I cannot relax
It's Saturday night, and I can now climax.

That one

I'm looking for that one
The man that wants to see me fulfill my mission
Instead of feeling me in the missionary position
One who will protect
One who commands respect
The man that knows God's plan
Who is not afraid to take a stand
I am alone –singular
I am refined – spectacular
I know what I deserve

I look across the room and see nothing
Nothing and no one
It's just me
Everyone in their own world and I am standing here
Waiting for him
Waiting for him to notice me
To see me
To know I exist
I don't know him, but I know he is here
I know we are supposed to meet tonight
This is the place
I can feel his breath on my shoulder
I turn around, and I see no one
There stands a waitress and a child

No men – No love
I am watching
Do I look as lost as I feel
Can he tell I am waiting for him
Is it I am being to obvious
I turn to the right and to the left
Again I force a conversation
Please notice me
Please see me
I am standing here in front of you
Tall, strong, proud, and available
Not free
Not open
Not needy
Just available
I know what I want
I know what I need
I know he is here in this room
Tonight
What is keeping us apart
Is it her, him, who is the cause of my anguish
I look up, and I hear a voice
Excuse me can I speak with you for a moment
My heart pounds
This must be him
He is tall, gorgeous, and articulate
He is perfect
He speaks and his words so beautiful are poisoned
He is a polished devourer

Not You

He asked to take me places only we have gone
If I look close I can still see the imprint of your hands on my skin
If I swallow hard I can still taste you
One deep inhale and your scent awakens my passion's passions
He could never take me there
His words danced like a perfect waltz between my thighs
My mind reminded me of your tongue coaxing open my intimacy
He offered immediate relief
You gave me intensity
How dare he try to make me forget you
My lady will never forget
She still holds your form as if she was molded especially for you
My breast tingle for you
They swell for you
My heart races for the taste of love you once gave
My heart has not forgotten
How could he not understand
She will never let him in her chamber
Your name tattooed on her walls
He was the words but not the magic
You have everything she, I ever wanted
Tonight my legs still tremble at the thought of your power
My skin still tingles at the very hope of another grand appearance
I want you, not him
As he described our strong approaching I could only picture you

I want you, not him

You are who my thoughts deliver when I close my eyes

I want him, not you

What we were, we were

I want him, not you

Problem, you don't want me

---do you?

LOVE'S CONFUSION

Our Love is Like the Last Day of Summer

Oddiscy is stared out the window while waiting for her man to come visit. During their last conversation, they discussed whether what they had was temporary heat or life-long warmth. Oddiscy sat on

the couch, legs crossed, arms cupped, feeling the hot summer sun on her face. She realized that summer is almost over. In the same instant, she realized how excited she was about the leaves changing and the fashions arriving with the autumn breeze. She is looking forward to the crisp morning breeze on her face. Yet, she knew the breeze will grow colder, and she will soon miss all the heat. Oddiscy wondered if her love with him was the same. Is their love going to end as hot and spicy as it started? She was not feeling sexy. She did not want to embrace anyone or anything but her feelings. Oddiscy was looking for answers. Would she know before he pulls in the driveway? Was he her summer fling or her Midnight Moon?

One thing Oddiscy learned early in life was that you will never know what a man is thinking unless you ask. This time she found herself caught in a dark place. She did not know what she wanted. She was not sure if she wanted the relationship to continue. A hot romance morphed into a comfortable relationship. She longed to be caressed. She needed to be tasted. Oddiscy craved a taste of the sweet and salty pleasure their relationship had long ago forgotten.

That morning she awakened him by gently sliding beneath the covers while he was sleep. Taking a warm soft cloth, she stroked him until her moaned. While he pretended to sleep, she kissed his inner thigh – left and then right. Repeating *the action again, except with a sexy nibble, she sighed as her hands relished in her own wetness. He was <u>erect</u>. Her mouth was full. Tip to base, she licked. She sucked. She felt his veins as the pulsated on his gorging member. He grabbed at the sheets. He grabbed for her head beneath the sheets. One hand on her bobbing head and one hand grasping at the headboard, he watched as she used her tongue as a paintbrush. He felt the warmth of her lips colliding with the crisp morning air. Impulsively, he yanked the cover off revealing her naked body.*

Face down. Ass in the air. Lower back arched. Hands pleasing herself. Oddiscy continued. Head down – eyes up. As he looked in her eyes – he could resist no longer – he exploded in her mouth. Oddiscy was not quite sure what made her take matters into her own hands...and mouth. Flipping over on her back, she softly, with two fingers, wiped her mouth. Those two fingers found themselves between her legs. Deeper. Further. In and Out. He watched as she squirmed. He watched as she pushed his hand away. He listened as she moaned and sighed with increasing pleasure. Grabbing her hands and holding them against the mangled, wet Egyptian cotton sheets, he thrust himself in her with a desire she never felt from him. He wanted every part of her. He devoured her from the inside. He wanted to know what she was thinking, feeling, wanting. No words. No directions. Just maddening passion.

No one went to work that day. Very few words were spoken. Each look landed them in another position. Each position led them to another room in the house. Dogs barked. The doorbell rang. The phone shattered the silence. Like the phone, Oddiscy wanted to be answered. Unlike the phone, she never signaled a request. They sat down to a simple dinner: grilled salmon topped with toasted almonds, jasmine rice, and steamed spinach. For dessert: Angel food cake topped with a blueberry sauce and whipped cream. As they sipped their after-dinner cocktail, he reached for her hand. He asked, "What was today?" Her reply...

Our love is like the last day of summer
We are excited about the change in seasons
We anticipate the new colorful landscape
Yet, we fear the cold, harshness that is inevitable

We look forward to rolling in the leaves
Ignoring the necessity of gathering and disposing of the same
Our hearts stare out the window as we cuddle awaiting snowfall
Never wanting to leave the warmth only our bodies can create

Will our love be lost in the cold?
Will we become so mesmerized by color that we lose focus on one another?
Will the snow numb us to harsh realities?
Is our love only a one season, hot, humid, only when the sun is shining type of love?

We question every kiss
We reminisce about hot action and loud laughter
Trips around the world took place without ever leaving town
Yet, we stand here wondering what's next - if anything

Do we have to end with the hot summer wind?
Does our love have to fade as the weather cools?
Will we be just another story to never forget - until next summer's love?
Is this a caliente good-bye?

Inquisitions and paranoia will take our passion to its grave
Summer never ends
It's always summer somewhere
We only need to go there, be there, live in eternal heat there

Our love is like the last day of summer
It's time for school to take us to the next level
There is no way to escape what we know
No way effectively to resist learning more

I have no answers for the future
If it's all over today, I will put on my coat and step proudly away
If it lasts into the next season, I will keep the fire lit only for you
All I know is this is the last day of summer and I'm still here.

This Love is Dangerous!

Your eyes are dangerous!
As they twinkle, my thighs glisten.
Your smile is dangerous!
As your lips part, so do my legs.
Your arms are dangerous!
I cannot help but grab them, pulling you deeper… into…my… heart.
Your hands get me into trouble I never what to escape.
Your fingers slide my lips open revealing my…tongue.

This love is dangerous!
In the moment, that moment, we meld into one inseparable being.
One hot, passionate being… giving, taking, sharing.
Did you hear the clashing of our heavens?
Did you hear the thunderous applause as the waters fell on our flesh?
Can you feel the fire threatening to consume our souls?
Do you feel my life as you penetrate the core of… my… heart?
Moments become hours as we refuse to yield to the limitations of time.
Our needs became our wants, which became our desires, which *come…* as our destiny.

This love is dangerous!
Syllables never become words as we try to speak.
Rise and fall, fall, and rise, as I struggle to take in your…breath.
I cannot breath alone, my breast smothered in sheets of sensuality!
I cannot see through the blinding light created by our simultaneous…

inescapable… explosions!

I can…not…give into to the confines of this world!

You are all I can feel, see, taste, smell, touch, know in this moment.

You are the man..infestation of every secret craving of my sexuality.

The more I give the more you want, the more I want the more…so much more..
you give.

This love is dangerous!

Heat awakens us!

Climax excites us!

Wetness invigorates us!

Creativity frees us!

Friction empowers us!

Compulsion drives us!

Hunger satisfies us!

Culmination soothes us!

This Love is Dangerous!

LOVE'S COLLISION

Love Has Its Own Direction

> *Love has its own direction. A path revealed when its direction is real, and the feeling is mutual. Until that time, its direction is blissful misdirection leaving you unfocused on his or her love.*

That one complacent tear in the right corner of my
eye Not moving not yielding to the healing cry
It dries leaving a stain
It lubricates once again
It has your name

This tear contains all my love for you
My passion is encased like frozen dew
It tries to move
But just like you
It is blocking my view

I cried once not knowing why
I looked to your picture and released a silent sigh
The tear came back
Showing me the love I lacked
Blitzed by an emotional attack

Unfamiliar Familiarity

I remember a guy that was so unfamiliar to me, yet I found in him familiar feelings. I tried to reconcile the feelings to the man. I could not. I want so badly for him to be the one; so, I tried to love him. He had a way about him that conjured of dormant feelings of lust and shameless eroticism. Late night flights. High-end hotels. Best restaurants. Smooth wine that caressed the throat and inhibited shyness. A perfect gentleman, he was well groomed and well dressed. I knew it was not love. But, I figured it was close enough. I know I am not the only one who has experience the entrapments of "right now love." I thought I could try to convince myself that it was real love. Really, I cannot even say it was lust. It was a moment in time. It lasted the length of an old love song playing repeatedly until a point where the song just faded away. The tune goes on and so does time. This love lingered for no time at all. I walked away eventually giving little thought to him. I am engulfed in the memories only when I when I hear his songs.

Oddiscy always had a thing for those involved in music. This one was no different.

He was a music maker like many of the men in my life. His music seemed to mimic the notes flowing from my soul. I could not be sure really because the notes of my soul seemed to change so often. With each musician came a new tune. For a time, I was not sure I was finding mutuality in them or if my heartbeat synchronized upon meeting them. For some reason, this man, this music man strummed a chord that changed my life. He was a placeholder, a pause, a moment of noisy silence. So, I understand him to be the one who played a tune that was temporarily real and permanently wrong. I can still hear his voice, his tone, and his songs anytime I want. I can still hear the feeling…

Unfamiliar Familiarity

From the moment we met, I felt a strange attraction
Maybe it was the look into your engaging eyes
The look that after each encounter leaves me with anticipation
Knowing your visits are only long enough for heated hi's and goodbye's
I want to know the man behind the mystery
The one who creates in me a new arousal
A longing to know you socially, physically, and musically
More than just the sensual and the sexual
Comfortable with your firm masculinity
If I am not careful, I could get lost in the strength of your arms
Wanting more, I am trapped by sensibility
Brief satisfaction that will cause no harm
Alarmed by my unfamiliar feelings
Not yet falling but eager to see where this will land
Who's touch leaves me smiling
For who is still an unfamiliar man

I wanted to get to know him from a distance. I longed for the feeling of love. I did not find it. Like Vidal Sassoon jeans of the '80's, his essence clung to me. I was more than happy to please him - he was acted as if he was privileged to please me. But, I knew his lifestyle did not match mine. I knew he only tolerated stories of my children. Neither of us cared to exchange more than small talk. We were polite. He told me his full name. I regret that I acted as if I did not care. He had his issues, but he was a gentleman. I appreciate him for not treating me the way I way treating him. I appreciate him for not treating me the way I expected to be treated. He was a remarkable distraction. When we faded, I rejected an impromptu meeting, there were no feelings of broken attachments. I had only the feeling of losing overwhelmingly pleasurable sex. It was fun…

Anyone can give me sex
But it takes a special man to give me pleasure
A certain man to release my stress
A different man to love and treasure

When can I see you again?

When can I see you again?

Baby, I miss you tonight.
I want to be with you tonight.
I need to tonight.
To just hold me tight.
I sit, and I wonder what we could have been
I miss your smile and the dimple on your chin
Baby I loved you
Will I ever love again?
Doing all the things the preacher said was a sin
In all of to use years, what have we gained
What we had -- unnamed
Made me a woman
Unloved and untamed
Free
I'm taking back my heart key
Can't escape it, I miss you to the nth degree
Tears you don't deserve to see
Thanks, I love the new me
What we had was a fallacy
A lie
We both refused to try
So we both know the answer to why
I just that one more question before I say goodbye

When can I see you again?

I can still feel your lips pressed against mine
Hear all the times you told me it would all be fine
But it's not
I used to say you are all I got
But you're not
I used to say the sex was hot
But it's not
I used to think I was happy
But I forgot
Now, I remember
Why were not together
Why, I'm alone
Without you have grown
A life without drama
Has set a new tone
Life is a reconfigured zone
Now, I'm focused
Seeing life as more than just us
Giving love it's final notice
Looking for closure
An end
We can never be lovers
You can never be my friend
But I need one more night before my new life can begin
So answer my question

When can I see you again?
Last time you called your voice made me tingle
I can't believe I went through all this to end up single
And confused
You took my love
Used and abused
But I'm healing
Peeling off layers of anger I was concealing
Only to find
I need you one more time
With you, I'm the one last bump
One last grind
One last pump from behind
Then we can go our own separate way
Then for real
Everything will be okay
So are you going to answer that question
What do I chalk this up as another lesson
Whatever your answer I'm not stressing
So take your time. I'm not pressing
Either way, we are over
After this question

When can I see you again?

LOVE'S
CONFESSIONS

If the World Only Knew

It is my secret wish to escape into your escape into me
To walk away from everything there is, while walking together with you
If the world knew how I felt, it would immediately halt its spin
It would deepen its tilt and shift its horizon all for us

I quietly await the moment our moistened palms meet
Fingers searching for the pulse which will decide the next dance
If the world understood how I long for you, it would darken its skies
Allowing only the light from the glow of my heart and your smile

I close my eyes in anticipation of the second you look deeper into my look
A look our eyes are incapable of seeing and so strong our heart almost cannot
bear
If the world could see how you feel for me, it would stop time at high noon
It would slow the clock at midnight to allow our uninterrupted love making

Every heartbeat quickens at the thought of you thinking of me thinking of you
Each thought leading back to the other and a connection from one another
If the world could hear our hearts, it would silence every thunderstorm
The world would refuse to mute the boom of our hearts, but allow the cooling
rain

It is my secret wish as I await for the moment I will await no more, to sing for
you
To reach a note so high only love could create during a seemingly endless
song

If the world knew this feeling, this longing, this look, this heart, this song, it would stop
It would stop everything it is doing to give us time to do everything we ever wanted to do

Running In Place

Everything I do has but one purpose,
To keep me from thinking of you.
I evade memories of your laughter
With menial daily choirs.
I elude the ever present hope of your smile,
By escaping into places of literary love.

I am running from you!
I run from the thought of you!
My feet carry me far beyond the essence of you!
Yet I sit writing of you.

There is no tomorrow free of my desire;
A desire which gripped my soul the day we met.
Will I one day stumble on an antidote
Freeing me from this splendid disease?
I am not at ease with my preoccupation.
I cannot explain its source or reason.

I keep running from you!
I run to locations hoping to escape the hope of you!
My legs grow weak as my heart strings are stretched from you!
Yet I sit and write more of you.

I cannot account for your overwhelming effect on me.

With each inhale, I try to take in some deep off-putting truth.
I secretly hope and fear the truth will unshackle my thoughts,
Surrendering them to their previously unassigned roamings,
But, I know they would only return like sad little pets
Seeking the love of home's arousal of comfort.

I am running far from you!
I run close to the arms of another but cannot because of you!
My thighs burn as I put miles of distance between my lips and you!
Yet I sit here and write tirelessly of you.

This is the realest fantasy I have lived.
Or, should I say yet to live.
In my dream, you are my reality.
In every moment of awakened reality, you are my dream.
You have stroked the alcoves of my mind
Never touching even, the smallest portion of my flesh.

I run and run and run from you!
I am running with passion from the passion connected to you!
My stomach aches from the increasing hunger for you!
Yet I sit silently smiling in one place as I write of you.

I want to know the weakness which gave you your strength.
You stand upright, forever erect, in my mind.
Your hands are an extension of your words which have already left me naked.
My hope is that you hope I will in time belong to you.
How do I reveal the invisible me?
How do I turn these feelings into memories?

I run again and again as far as I can from you!
I am running with the intensity of threatened sensuality which could cripple if I
came near you!
My heart throbs become silence as my arms slice through the air propelling my
escape from you!
Yet I sit with legs crossed writing of you.

You see me, but do you feel my presence?
Do you know my tongue rolls softly across my lips at the moistening thought of
you?
You threaten my satisfaction with happiness,
Which offers endless satisfaction.
I reach for you from an increasing distance
Resigned to wait for you to no longer wait for me.

I run and stop and run and run from you!
I am running as fast as my shyness will take me, but unchanged are the scenes
and scents of you!
My smile reaches out into the expanse of space for you!
Yet I sit running in place writing of you!

Midnight Move

You awaken something in me that I did not know was sleep
Your words touch me in places I was not sure anyone could reach
There is something enticing about your powerful gentleness
That makes me wonder about the intensity of your caress
Whether God meant this for right now or maybe for more
I am grateful for you and excited to see what God has in store
It is too soon to know the design or the whole plan
But, one thing I do know, I like the view from where I stand
You have inspired me to write, to want to trust, to want to love
I can see in you a greater greatness, a special outpouring of God's love
When it comes to you, there is so much new about the way I feel
So many answers I trust time and God will reveal
I never overlook the importance of passion and chemistry
So, I do wonder how that first kiss will be
These are my midnight thoughts as I think of you
The next move is for you to do

Chambered Heart

There's a part of her that wants to be with you
A part of her that wants to be next to you
A part of her that has to be a part of you
And still a part of her that knows it cannot be you

At first meeting, she knew you were inaccessible
That her love in return would be unavailable
She went against the rules and against her principles
She fell into a love that was all but criminal

Trying to convince herself it was only lust
She opened her heart with too much trust
Having you in her life was a definite must
Her secret until her body is dust

She can see your eyes without seeing your face
The sound of your voice takes her to a hidden place
In her mind, your every feature she could trace
Can she have one night of grapes, wine, and lace

How she truly felt she could not describe
Too shy to tell you how she felt your vibe
Her heart dancing to the drum of an ancient tribe
She had no choice but to enlist a scribe

It is not my duty to analyze what she feels
Nor, is it my place to remove her ceiling
There is so much she should be revealing
Just a glimpse into what she's concealing

There's a part of her that wants to be with you
A part of her that wants to be next to you
A part of her that has to be a part of you
And still a part of her that knows it can't be you

Missing the Unknown

My heart awaits a man I have never
met A name I have not heard
A face I have never seen
I miss the touch I never felt
When we meet, I will know him

I search the world for a hint
Looking to see if he misses me too
Is he in the crowd?
When did he loose me?
When he meets me, he will know me?

My memory conjures up a shadow
My ears can hear his voice
My nose can smell his scent
My arms long for his embrace
When I meet him, I will know him?

I stand here in this crazy world
Trying to be a constant presence
I miss the man who never met me
Is it who will awaken my love?
When we meet, we will know us

Our spirits were created a pair

No one can take your place
I miss your manly stance
As if my heart has known it for
years, I miss my unknown love

I miss him even though we have never met. It is as if my heart knows who he is, but life has not introduced us. What does this mean? Who is this man? I am so excited to meet him. It feels as if I will wake up tomorrow and he will be standing there. I am not sure what I will give to him, nor what he will give me. I am missing him like he has been on a long trip, and these are the moments before he returns home.

Attention is what I need
It's what my heart seeks
Loneliness disguised

The Man

You are the man I always wanted to want
The hand I always wanted to hold
The lie I always wanted to tell
There is nothing about you that is real
No part of your body I cannot feel
I cannot stop wanting you to be my truth

I do not know you, but I feel my soul met you before
There was some distant time where we danced across life's floor
Arms crossed against my chest, I am holding on to you
I hold on to the image I have never seen
I hold on to the heart I never felt beat
You are the ideal man

The insanity of it all grips my heart
I can hear your laughter at the jokes I am soon to tell
I can feel the kiss you have yet to give
You are the man crafted for me
The man no one but the Creator can see
Not reincarnated this will be our first time

It Wasn't the Time

The dream I had and never knew
The flower I watered that never grew
The look in his eyes when I could not decide
The silent words that my lips never tried
He rubbed my shoulder and kissed my forehead
I held his waist and wished his thoughts were said
It wasn't the time
My heart knew it wasn't the time

I felt his eyes tell me the story
Why my prize wasn't his glory
It happened too soon for his heart to absorb
I would settle secretly to adore
He is my hidden treasure
I am his secret pleasure
It wasn't the time
My heart knew it wasn't the time

The hope of the tomorrows even today cannot imagine
The blade of grass in a meadow refusing to blend in
The strength in our laughter that rejects every fear
The smile in my heart that chokes back every tear
He caressed me softly as none before him
He separated himself from the rest of them
It wasn't the time

My heart knew it wasn't the time

Now I sit settled on waiting
Where is the harm in love contemplating?
Who is the decider of when the time is right?
Who gets to choose when our meetings are no longer at night?
He held my hand gripping my heart
I rub his hand wondering if this was the start
It wasn't the time
My heart wants to know why it wasn't the time.

THINKING OF YOU

First Impression

Is it me, or, is he really that mesmerizing?
Could it be that he really had me at first meeting?
Or did it happen at that first word?
I attribute it to heartfelt mutterings of the absurd.
The heart speaks of his unknown masculinity.
The mind challenges his true spirituality.
Yet my eyes cannot erase his vision.
Has he coaxed me into submission?
His hands were so strong in that moment.
His face speaks of a story, not so recent.
There is a bond between the unexplained,
Hope for the passion once untamed.
He is a glimpse of destiny's voice.
Question is: Will I be his choice?
No, I will not walk this unforgotten path
Looking closely at what I wished would last!
I try desperately to forget his soul!
Ignoring the yearning my skin does hold!
There is still something impure about his purity.
Something insane about his sanity
It is in his imperfection that I am enticed.
Of his upright selection I wonder, will it suffice?
But I know this is not true lust.
Meeting, seeing, speaking to him again is a must!
I daydream about his daily tasks

Images of his playful boyhood past.
I stand with my hand to my cheek
Contemplating the brown man, tall and sleek
This is all happening in my mind!
Nothing has yet to happen in real time!
He is no longer there where we met.
His walk, Egyptian in every respect
Now treads the sands of my imagination.
Will he walk out my mind and in my life?

Unfocused Focus on Your Love

Unfocused focus on your love
Or lack there of
Zoned in on your tone
Hypnotized by your voice on the phone
But that is just me lost in lovin'
Wishing you loved me back and
All I can focus on is the unfocused view of you

You are the vision my eyes hope to see
Blinded by the fear we will never be
They find clarity in love
Yet can't focus on the reality of rising above
The truth that there is no "we"
Just the truth of me

Eyes that have a heart of their own
Ears that echo a constant sensual groan
A mouth that forms the words of the unspoken
My senses must be jokin'
Foolin' me in to believing you could
Ever be the this clever
To fool me
Into this unreal reality

The way you touch me contradicts "goodbye"

The way you look at me says anything, but love is a
lie Then there is the way you ignore me
There, I find the roots of reality's tree
Still trying to focus on my unfocused you
Now a dry tear shades my view

I find solitude in our togetherness
The hope of foreverness
Which is simply my what of escaping
Running away from the …

Proximity

Problem is I am sitting here thinking about you
Thinking about that moment and each moment after that
Trying to decide whether to change my focal view
When I am with you that's exactly where I want to be at
Nowhere else
With no one else
Just next to you

I can feel your hands even now
I just cannot forget
Slowly going even further down
And it's here I sit
Nowhere else
With no one else
Just close to you

Your voice is strong and powerful
Powerful enough to calm my water
Strong enough to allow me to be graceful
Your tone says there is only now, never later
Nowhere else
With no one else
Just near to you

Deeper I look into you - deeper inside

Through the past
Past the pain, you try to hide
Seeing the smile that I want to last
Nowhere else
With no one else
Just available to you

There is more to you than just your flow
More within I need to expose
I need to understand – I need to know
Why is it you this day my heart chose?
Nowhere else
With no one else
Just familiar to you

Problem is I am sitting here still thinking of you
Envisioning our next moment of propinquity
Deciding whether to change my peripheral view
Knowing my happiness is lost in our proximity
Nowhere else
With no one else
Just my heart to you

Verbal Night

His voice walked in and quieted me
Hushing my nighttime thoughts
The rumble of a thousand men sat beside me
Supplying the love once sought

His tone hummed a forceful silence
Leaving my ears in awe
Too few days trapped in this trance
It is golden what I saw

He spoke of nothing I would naturally note
Every word seared my heart
Syllable after syllable, I hold for hope
Each letter enchanted from the start

I could have listened the entire night
Applause trapped beneath my breast
His volume reached a reluctant height
"Okay, Goodbye" put me to rest.

Impact

There is one word that describes the moment we met – awakening.
Feelings I had resolved to lay to rest invigorated by the potency of your presence
Leaving the darkness of my past, I tried to suppress the hopes of a tomorrow
Then, I was mesmerized by the manifestation your smile.

My heart began to open like a young yellow rose living its first spring morning breeze
My hopes emerged like the piercing moonlight glowing through a cloudy summer's midnight
My fears faded into the background as you emerged as the star of my celestial stage
Then, I experienced the joyful spectacle of your smile.

I could tell you all the things I adore about you, but there are not enough words
I could relay my deepest feelings, but there is not enough time
I could tell you my greatest admiration – your passionate, caring soul
Then, I was met with the strength of your smile.

You conquer the world with the determination of a fearless queen
You pursue your goals as if there is no other option
You live the life of a lady refusing to settle for the limitations of less
Then, I was overwhelmed by the sweetness of your smile.

I marvel in the beauty of your ability to resist the impossible, accepting all as possible

You, a talented artist, identified a space and carved a place of which only you can fill
Not knowing the future, I made no predictions.
Then, I gave way to the intensity of your smile

As the sun rises each day, I am grateful for your existence
As the world turns, I appreciate your stability
As I look in your eyes, I hear the walls around my heart crumble
Then, I realize you are more than just your smile!

Wishes for a Special Friend

There is one guy that will always hold a memorable place in my heart. He had been my best friend even when I was his worst friend. We never quite get our friendship right, but it is understood that we are best friends. He treats me better than any man does. He is both loving and lovable. The lady that hooks him will indeed be blessed. I wrote this poem when there was a moment that I thought our lives were taking us in separate directions. It was in that moment that I thought I would never see him again. He did not allow space or time to be the death of a friendship. He gave me the glimpse into how a man should treat a lady. He opens doors. He allows me to order first. He reminds me that when I find that special man and that special man finds me, I am to be treated with love and respect. I am worth more, not worthless.

You are a friend so special to me
I wish life gives you the best there can be
I pray God directs you to where the next path lies
Allowing you to see life through His eyes
May every dream, hope, and vision come true

I wish for your success in everything you do
Deep within, may your forgotten passions resurrect
So, tomorrow brings more than today expects
It is in the smallest faith that lays your biggest victory
It is your biggest hope that gives life its simplicity
May the music in your soul resonate like never before
And the windows of Heaven open with every closed door
Please know every phase in life requires many steps
I pray your fading past allows you to focus on what's next
Seeing clearly your goals without limitation
Pursuing your best without delay or reservation
Remember God can transform mistakes into breaks
And give you patience when life refuses to wait
May your pleasures in life never end
These are my wishes for a special friend.

ANGRY PASSION

I Write for Me

I write this for me!
Not for you to see.
Not words you need to read.
I write this strictly, solely for me!
I write this because my heart bleeds.
Because my world has crashed down
Because I cannot interpret my own
thoughts, I write this poem for me!
My soul needs this written.
My heart needs to be heard.
My mind needs to declare freedom!
This is why I write this – for me!
You want my words to grab your heart.
My words to bring you to tears
My words to answer unasked questions
How dare you steal my words?
Use the for your pleasureful gain
Encase them in your memory
I take back my words, you pirate
You will no longer pillage my thoughts
Your access to my emotions is denied
I write this, whatever this is, for me
I write what my own emotions dare to say
I write what my life is missing
I write of yesterdays yet to happen

So much taken, but my words are my own
You hear them, but you will never <u>own</u> my words
I write, I write, I write…. For me!

Heart Drop

I can feel the tears dripping from the depths of my heart
One drop, two, three, drop after drop
Every second led me to this eternity
I am crying so deep within I cannot reach the tears to wipe them
There are no arms long enough to console me
Each tear has a name and a face
Each name was once tattooed, with fire, on my heart
Now the faces, liquefied, course through my veins and out my pours
The pressure and heat of the world cause the tears to evaporate before they can
fall
I have fallen, yet again
My knees buckle and ankles fold, pulling me closer to the bottom
I use my hand to break my fall
Only to realize I only slowed my decent
Heartbroken once again

Tell the Truth

Was that a stolen moment?
Was it not me but the setting?
Was it a kiss or a reaction?
Tell the truth!

Is this the end of our friendship?
Is this the beginning of our future?
Is this the middle of confusion?
Tell the truth!

Are you going to remain silent?
Are you going to speak your mind?
Are you going to fight your fear?
Tell the truth!

Where is the resting place of your heart?
Where is the hope of our future?
Where is the trust in our sight?
Tell the truth!

When did you decide to be undecided?
When did you choose that I am the chosen?
When did you opt to ignore me?
Tell the truth!

Why are these questions necessary?
Why are these questions conflicted?
Why are these questions all I have?
Tell the truth!

The truth is not what I anticipated
The loudest word often silent
Through actions, it's emancipated
My heart, I am afraid, is not as resilient

My heart walks to the truth, in fear of the truth, wanting the truth, hiding the truth, hidden in the truth, relying on the truth, to cover its lies in the truth that creates the truth - not manifested in a hope for truth all while running from the truth!

Does love exist?
Tell the truth!

Thoughts of an Unmarried Wife

> **YOU GOT ALL THE ANSWERS TO NONE OF THE QUESTIONS**
> **ALL OF THE OUTCOMES TO NONE OF THE PROBLEMS**
> **TRAPPED IN A TRI-STATE**
> **LOST IN A MIND STATE**
> **LIFE STUCK ON WAIT**

In search of fulfillment, I found none
Not looking for the only, but the everyone
Not sure when all this begun
Not sure if it could ever be done

Walking the line of lonely insanity
Love seems to be simply my fantasy
Just one gentleman romancing me far from my past or present reality

Who are you? They never want to know
A woman mature, I too must grow
I, too, possess love juices that flow
Like a yo-yo I throw hold throw

Lending myself to occasional pleasures
Lowering the value of my absolute treasures
Refusing to allow names to define or measure
Knowing I am what I am not my leisure

I deny my state of denial
Accepting the unacceptable is not my style
I know there is someone who can with me walk this mile
Reoccurring aloneness my lifelong trial

What is the cloaked man's name?
From a child's heart, I am a woman exclaimed
Is he the fighter of my battles or the winner of a game
Or maybe I am the one who cannot be tamed?

Trying to figure the truth in all this
Why life is enjoyed when taking risks
Erratic behavior yields temporary bliss
Trapped in a world between misses and miss

Useless Man, Don't Bother

Sentences
Phrases
Words
Syllables
Such ignorance and laziness should be criminal
Love
Joy
Respect
Happiness
To you useless
Wake up
Rise up
Live up
Look up
Such ignorance and laziness should be criminal
Be a man
A role model
A father
A mentor
You resent this
I gave
I give
You have emptied my cup
I bowed to you
Repent to who

Sorry for what
Don't bother, time's up

How Long Must I Sleep?

Hottest of Showers and crispest of sheets
Under the blankets I sleep
I want to sleep until this life is over
Not my life, I want to live on
But, this life, all that is right now, is over
How long must I sleep?
How long must I sleep until darkness fades?
How long before my life becomes a memory
Before it is all over and new life begins
I want to keep sleeping, slumbering
Until my present fades into memories
Until the dreams of the future become my reality
How long must I sleep for that to happen?
Will I awaken in an eternal place?
Will I open my eyes in a distant
millennium? How long must I sleep?
Or, will I awaken next year, next month?
Will my eye pop open next week?
Will the sleep be short, like a nap?
Is it possible I will awaken in minutes?
Could it all be over in minutes?
How long, I pray, must I sleep?
I cannot bear this life!
Yet, I do not wish to leave it!
Sitting as a spectator in the theatre of my own life

I wait for the next act, the next scene
Such an intolerable show
I close my eyes, head back of course
I want to sleep
Awaken me, my friend, when the good part comes
Should there be no more good
Awaken me when it's over
For now, I want to sleep
For now, I want to dream
For now, I want to forget now
How long must I sleep for me to disappear?
For my true self to appear in bliss?
Is there no date marked on the calendar?
Is there no suggestion of timing?
How long, I ask, must I sleep?
However long I close my eyes
I will keep them closed for as long as it takes
No sunlight, no Moon will my eyes see
No pain, no joy will my heart feel
I will sacrifice the beauty to destroy the pain
Believing one day I will awaken
In this very life I am living
I will awaken happy and strong
My dreams will truth
The hunger will fade
The loneliness will disappear
I want to sleep, slumber, nap
Minute by minute until it happens
How long must I sleep?

Crying Tears

Today I am crying
My eyes are dry
I am crying
My lips curl up into a smile
Cheeks with a hint of sun-kissed blush
My arms hug

Today I am crying
Despite the happiness that surrounds
I am crying
Laughter echoing through sighs
Playful attitudes piercing my emotions
Hands clap

Today I am crying
My love reaches
I am crying
My hope infiltrates the heart
Joy in its absence is contagious
My silence yells

Today I am crying
There is no reason
I am crying
Because my heart is alone

Because my path is hidden
Because I am

Today I am crying
My tears are invisible
I am crying

Yielding to Conclusions

Opening an eye to a false truth
Recognizing a hidden view lost in youth
Looking glass into the future lessons
Comatose in and out blinded visions
Lost in a world of compromising lust
Who can fight the mounting odds
Who can get through the sea of No's and Nods
Yesterday's love becomes tomorrow's regret
Right or wrong does not matter
In the end life is all but scattered
Future so bright it blinds as the sun
Point before one decides want or want none
Decisions \Choices based insight and intuition
Fate Destiny sends us on a long life mission
Conclusions yielded views yield choices yield conclusions

REFLECTION

DEEP

Deep is the strength of my intelligence
Deep is the destination of my love
Deep is the level of my complexity
Deep is the power of my God above

Deep is the man that respects himself
Deep is the man that cares for the child
Deep is the man who clings to his hope
Deep is the man that understand a lady's smile

Deep are the desires for your desire
Deep are the rivers of my emotion
Deep are the pains that led to my joy
Deep are the depths of my devotion

Precious memories

Precious memories in twined in tarnished dreams
Treasures forgotten in attics lost or so it seems
Loving hugs - harsh words - kisses and hits
Go deeper still remember the smiles not the split lips
Scenes flicker some fade, but memories are just that
Can you see the first ride or do you see the first flat
Walks in the park, lonely benches, kids playing, and loud cries
God has blessed the worst memory of all, the death of a son
He changed it into a chance to see eternal life begun
Death and suffering brought healing and power
Don't let your tarnished dreams your precious memories devour.

Todays

It is the todays that make me long for yesterday
It is the yesterdays that make me fear tomorrow
Where is the day when pain begins to fade
And joy can finally swallow sorrow

Praying

I have walked this path many times before
It ends the same way
My head down and knees on the floor
Praying hard to be able to pray
For the end of this circular way

I stride down the path with baggage in tow
Carrying my fears, desires, and faith
In an embellished bag so no one will know
I continue rather than leave it to fate
Fearing what will happen if I decide to wait

To the Hills I'm Left to Be

Looking to the hills lost in its shadows
Overpowered by the very force meant to free me
Yet I stand, eyes up, lips pursed, head toward heaven's windows
There is no place left to be

I want to strive, to grow, to understand
But, the hills want too much from me
Still in search of the desired plan
But somehow it is all left to be

This is the day the hills walk closer
Allowing the inhabitant to stand with me
I stepped back further
Wanting just to be, left to be

The hills have no fault
All the fault lies with me
Everything impure resides in my vault
Sealed no longer left to be

I look to the hills where I find help
 From those hills no longer a stranger to me
In search for the love, I never felt
In His arms, I'm left to be

I am more concerned

I am more concerned
I am more concerned with your heart than your color
I am more concerned with your vision than your reality
I am more concerned with your love than your sexuality
I am more concerned with your hope than your fears

I am more concerned

I am more concerned with your future than your past
I am more concerned with your honor than your words
I am more concerned with your education than your entertainment
I am more concerned with your legacy than your longevity

I am more concerned

I am more concerned with your peace than your possessions
I am more concerned with your purpose than your plan
I am more concerned with your vision than your sight
I am more concerned with your power than your privilege

I am more concerned

I am more concerned with your freedom than your bondage
I am more concerned your heartbeat than your heartbreak
I am more concerned with your greatness than your lack

I am more concerned with your assets than your liabilities

I am more concerned

I am more concerned with you than what others say about you
I am more concerned with you than what others did to you
I am more concerned with you than what others took from you
I am more concerned with you than what others told you

I am concerned...not worried!

The Power of Nothing!

My voice called out to you, begging
Your ears heard the intensity in every vibrating
syllable, yet you did nothing
You looked in my eyes, gave me a smile
And did nothing

I am not the forgotten,
I am the ignored
You saw me in need of empowerment
You saw I was undereducated
Yet you did nothing

I could see the lack of concern in your eyes
I could hear your dismissive words
I asked for nothing
You gave me a firm handshake and a promise to return
You have me a fleeting moment of hope

I chased you down as if you were my last
chance, I peeped behind every corner of every
dead-end
You continued to hide your talent in the highest places
Places I could not reach without your help
You did nothing

Like everyone before you,

I was left disappointed
The next step was unknown
So, I did nothing
You glanced over giving me a smile

I leapt up and ran to you
You smiled again
Realizing I was not the recipient
I turned and once again did nothing
You, seeing my dismay, did nothing

Two roads of nothingness converging
Productivity wasted
Intelligence set aside
I did nothing
You did nothing

We are the same!

This Gift I Give to You

The spirit of Christmas in its pure state
For you, my gift I will translate

I give to you my most precious gift
One not found on any Christmas list
It is a gift meant to share
One you already had and weren't aware
I gift you my strength in these turbulent times
To use when your own strength you cannot find
I gift you my hope when mountains block your view
To use when despair overshadows you
I gift you my smile when life is at its best
To know I understand what it means to be blessed

I give to you my most precious gift
One not found on any Christmas list
It is a gift I am privileged to give
One that will help both of us live
I gift you my tears when you are too strong to cry
To use when you don't know the answer to "Why?"
I gift you my hug when you feel alone
To use when you feel loneliness is home
I gift you my laughter when you tell a joke
To know life is never too serious for a tickle or a poke

I give to you my most precious gift
One not found on any Christmas list
It is a gift meant to share
One you already had and weren't aware
I gift you my help when you don't want to ask
To use when the power of one can't complete the task
I gift you my loyalty when need a friend
To use whenever want – again and again
I gift you my pride when you succeed
To know I support you in word and in deed

~~~~

The spirit of Christmas in its pure state
For you, my gift I will translate

I give to you my most precious gift
One not found on any Christmas list
I gift you love as given to me
By Jesus, my Savior so abundantly

FAUX FINALE

I am Oddiscy. I will always be Oddiscy. When I look in the mirror, I love who I see. This is not the end. I will continue to search for more sensual truths, finding more pleasure in pleasure, more love in love, and even love locked away in pain.

Often, I am asked what lessons I learned when it comes to sex and relationships. My answer: Be yourself and give of yourself. Be equally willing to give love and receive love. Embrace passion, but not so tightly that you have to work too hard for release. Finally, do not discount the power of love. Give love freely, but do not be free with your love.

Remember, there is a distinct difference between touching and caressing. Make sure your special lover enjoys the benefits of your caress. Make sure you never settle for just being touched. Whether it is your skin or your heart, you deserve to be caressed.

Lips Closed
No one Knows
Hidden Quietly
Just Oddiscy!

www.ingramcontent.com/pod-product-compliance
Lightning Source LLC
Chambersburg PA
CBHW050948120626
46552CB00001B/437